First published in Dutch as *Drie wijzen uit het Oosten* by Christofoor in 2013
First published in English by Floris Books in 2014
© text and illustrations Loek Koopmans /Uitgeverij Christofoor, Zeist 2013
English edition © 2014 Floris Books
All rights reserved. No part of this publication may be reproduced without
the prior permission of Floris Books, 15 Harrison Gardens, Edinburgh
www.florisbooks.co.uk
British Library CIP Data available
ISBN 978-178250-135-0
Printed in Malaysia

The Three Wise Men

Loek Koopmans

Floris Books

Long, long ago, a very special star appeared in the night sky. It shone more brightly than all the other stars, and people shouted with excitement when they saw it. They pointed up at the sky, calling to their neighbours to come and look at it.

It was the most beautiful star that anyone had ever seen.

Far away, in a distant land, there were three wise men called Melchior, Caspar and Balthasar. They were stargazers. They knew the names of all the stars, and exactly where to spot them in the night sky. But they gazed at *this* star in wonder. They did not know the star's name. They had never seen anything like it before.

It was a miracle.

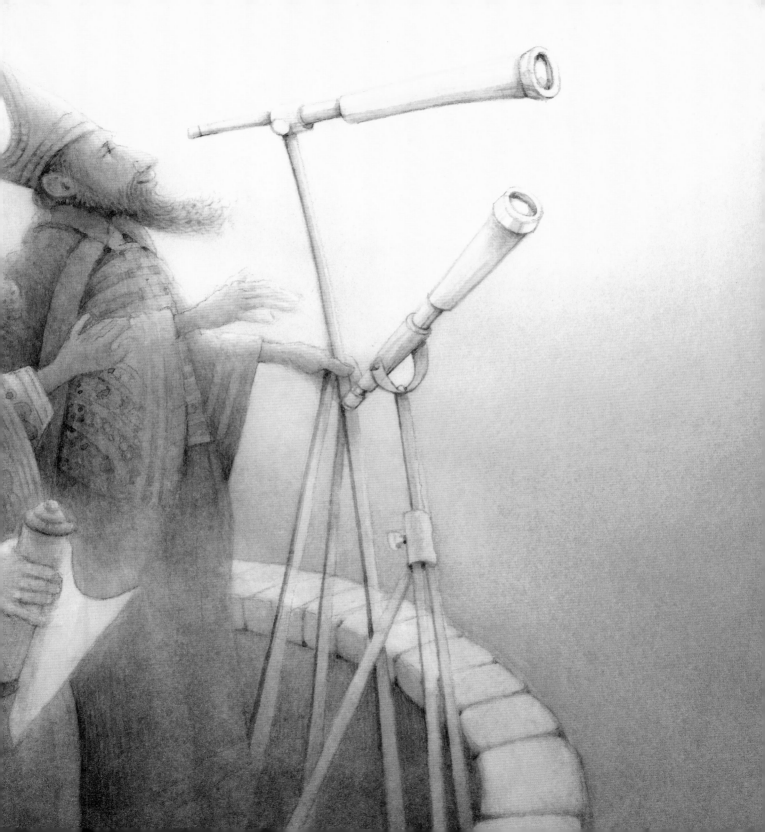

The three wise men wanted to know all about the beautiful new star. They thought long and hard, and made many calculations. Melchior peered through his telescope. Caspar searched in all his books. Balthasar scratched behind his ears.

Then they remembered an ancient story: that a bright star would appear in the sky as a sign that a new king had been born. Could this star mean there was a new king?

Melchior, Caspar and Balthasar decided they would
follow the mysterious star. Nobody could stop them.
They wanted to find out everything they could.

The three wise men bought three camels for their journey.
They knew they would have to travel on unmarked paths,
through deserts, over high mountains and across swamps.
They didn't know how long their journey would take,
so they packed plenty of food and water.

They agreed that if a new king had been born, they wanted to welcome him warmly, and bring him fine gifts.

So they bought the very best presents they could find: gold, and two special kinds of perfume called frankincense and myrrh.

They loaded their camels with clothes,
food and drink, blankets for cold nights and,
of course, the precious gifts.

In the evening, when the bright star appeared
in the sky once more, they said goodbye
to their families, and headed west.

They travelled past the borders of their own land and along unfamiliar paths, always following the shining star.

Even when it was daytime, and the star was no longer shining, the three wise men knew which route to take. They had no doubts. They felt full of joy and excitement.

Then, after many hours and days and nights, there it was. The beautiful star was right in front of them, twinkling and sparkling above a simple stable. The three wise men knew their journey had come to an end.

Melchior, Caspar and Balthasar climbed down from their camels.
Carefully and quietly, they walked towards the stable.

They tiptoed inside. There they saw an ox and a donkey, the father Joseph and the mother Mary, and the little baby in the manger. Everything was quiet and still.

Mary's baby was called Jesus, and he smiled up at the three wise men. Suddenly, everyone could hear the distant sound of angels singing.

Melchior, Caspar and Balthasar felt a
wonderful sense of peace and happiness.

They knelt by the manger and offered their
gifts to the infant: the beautiful gold, and the
sweet-smelling frankincense and myrrh.

The three wise men were full of joy. They knew that they would tell everyone about the special baby they had found in the peaceful stable.

And every time they shared the story, they would hear the sound of angels singing.